I0572415

Published by: Camistin Publishing

Camistin Publishing books are available anywhere books are available anywhere books are sold. Substantial discounts are available on bulk quantities to corporations, educational institutions, professional associations, and other organizations. Requests for support, reproduction and bulk sales may be made via email to support@camistin.com.

Paperback ISBN: 978-1-62408-013-5
eBook ISBN: 978-1-62408-014-2

Thank you for supporting Camistin Publishing, a veteran owned small business.

*For The Human Race, Their Eternal Progress
In Truth, Light, And Intelligence...*

Pure Human Female: An Alien's Cosmic Quest to Decode Earth's Most Mysterious Gender

By Vega Sparx

Prelude – A Note From The Publisher

It has been an extraordinary honor to work with Vega Sparx on his first book, Pure Human Female: An Alien's Cosmic Quest to Decode Earth's Most Mysterious Gender. You might be curious about how our partnership began and why Vega entrusted Camistin Publishing to serve as his exclusive partner. As a native of Las Vegas, I'd like to say it was chance that brought us together. Vega, however, sees it differently.

Our meeting happened during one of my usual runs in North Las Vegas—not just any run, but a deep dive into the tunnels beneath the city's bustling streets. For me, these runs were more than exercise; they were an exhilarating escape. I'd often sprint into the darkness with only the faintest light ahead, sometimes a flickering fire lit by those who called the tunnels home, other times a small glow marking the far end.

On this particular run, as I emerged from a tunnel leading to the untouched desert north of Vegas, I saw him—Vega Sparx. He looked like any ordinary person at first glance, but there was something indescribably different about him. He stood staring into the vast desert as though contemplating the universe itself.

Naturally curious, I approached him, and we struck up a conversation. From the *start*, Vega exuded a rare charm and an uncanny ability to live entirely in the present moment. Whether savoring breakfast, engaging in our conversations, or simply walking beside me, he radiated wonder, delighting in the world with the awe of a child seeing it for the first time. It was captivating.

During our chats, Vega asked me about my dreams. I shared how much I love writing and journaling and how I've long dreamed of helping others tell their stories. He listened intently, encouraging me to pursue my ambitions. Then he shared his story—a story that felt impossible, almost absurd. When he told me who he really was, I thought, Well, this friendship was too good to be true. But something deep inside nudged me to give him a chance.

Curiosity got the better of me, and I reached out to a trusted friend at the Las Vegas Metropolitan Police Department. That friend confirmed the strange details: unexplained body cam footage, a family claiming a UFO had crashed in their backyard, and even cameras set up to monitor the property. The more I investigated, the more I started to believe Vega's story.

As I came to know him better, I saw what can only be described as miracles. Vega Sparx has a message to share—a message for the world. And somehow, I've been lucky enough to help him tell it. Working with Vega has been a privilege and a journey I'll treasure forever.

This book, like Vega himself, is unique. It's raw, untouched by the conventions of mainstream publishing. I haven't imposed rigid rules or length requirements, nor have I polished it to fit industry expectations. My goal was simple: to preserve Vega's voice and let his words speak directly to you, the reader. We have changed the names of those referenced in Vega's interactions. We did not want to bring undue attention to their lives and have swarms of people flocking to them asking questions about Vega.

There were moments when I sought clarification, asking Vega questions that inspired minor revisions. Yet even then, Vega was adamant about leaving certain things untouched—"mistakes," he called them, though he assured me they had meaning. What that meaning is, only you can decipher.

So, dear reader, thank you for picking up this book. By doing so, you're not just embarking on a journey with Vega; you're helping a small family-run publishing company like mine scrape out a living. You're helping Vega continue to share his adventures and perspectives with the world.

I hope you'll approach this book with an open mind, a sense of wonder, and a willingness to laugh, learn, and reflect. Please enjoy Pure Human Female: An Alien's Cosmic Quest to Decode Earth's Most Mysterious Gender.

Introduction: Arrival and First Impressions

Greetings, Humans! My Earth name is Vega Sparx, and I hail from a planet far beyond your human understanding. On the night of April 30, 2023, my transportation system—one of the finest in the galaxy, I assure *you*—experienced a malfunction of epic proportions. I crash-landed in a place you call Las Vegas, in the state of Nevada. It was late, the desert air was cool, and little did I know, my arrival would cause quite a stir.

As I stumbled out of the wreckage, I found myself in someone's backyard, surrounded by curious glowing objects and odd plant life. Before long, bright lights appeared in the distance, accompanied by ancient transports emitting loud, wailing noises. Later, I learned these were called "police cars," responding to reports of "strange lights in the sky" and "unidentified beings." My plan to keep a low profile didn't survive my first hour on your planet *Mars,* I mean Earth.

Though I employed a few advanced cloaking techniques, I soon discovered that humans have an impressive arsenal of cameras. Some captured glimpses of me, and before I knew it, I became the subject of news headlines about an "alien visitation" in Las Vegas. So much for sneaking in unnoticed. First impressions, it seems, are hard to shake.

With my transportation beyond repair and no way to contact my home planet, I quickly realized I was stuck here—for now. My new mission became simple: survive, adapt, and, hopefully, find a way back home. Writing became my refuge—a way to process this strange world—and I've decided to share my reflections. After all, while I'm here and now that I can write in your English tongue, why not?

Wandering under the cover of darkness, I was lured into the city by its bright lights and lively sounds. Yet, unsure of my welcome, I sought refuge beneath the glittering surface, where I discovered a side of Las Vegas I doubt many tourists ever see. Beneath your bustling streets lies a hidden network of tunnels, home to many humans who have retreated from the world above. Here, I found shelter and anonymity. I wanted to be invisible, and in these tunnels, I fit right in.

It was there I encountered humanity in its rawest form. Some of my new acquaintances battled things called "addictions," which seemed to hold their minds and freedom captive. Others faced "mental illness," often exacerbated by chemicals or imbalances in their bodies. Still others had simply lost their homes and found kinship and shelter underground. These humans, despite their struggles, were kind enough to share their stories with me. They became my first teachers, and I am deeply grateful for each one of them.

Joe, a man with an old guitar and an unshakable spirit, introduced me to the wonders of music. His melodies stirred something deep within me—what you might call a "soul." Joe even taught me to play a few notes, and I've since composed some Earth-inspired songs that I hope to share with you one day.

Maria, a gentle woman with a knack for scavenging, taught me to read English using newspapers she had collected. Some of these papers featured images of Earth women wearing nothing but their human skin. I wondered if they got cold. Maria laughed when I asked and encouraged me to keep reading.

Then there was a man who showed me a business opportunity involving watches called "Rolex." We would acquire them for $30 each and sell them for $300 on the streets of Vegas. While our customers were initially delighted, one returned with rage in his eyes, claiming the watches weren't real. That's when I learned about something called "counterfeiting." Note to self: not all Earth commerce is honest.

Despite these lessons—some enlightening, others humbling—I found friendship and a sense of belonging among those who lived *in* the shadows. They shared their resilience, humor, and humanity with me, and I will always be thankful for their teachings.

As weeks turned into months, I realized that writing could help me make sense of everything I was experiencing. Perhaps my observations could even benefit others. This book is my first attempt to document and share what I've learned. My focus here is to explore one of Earth's most fascinating mysteries: the human female.

Coming from another world, I find your concepts of gender roles and biological sex both intriguing and perplexing. Earth women are extraordinarily diverse, and understanding their essence has become one of my greatest challenges—and joys.

My first foray into human society was, shall we say, a tad confusing. Eager to observe, I wandered into an establishment adorned with flashing signs and music that made my metaphoric antennas tingle. (I don't actually have antennas, but if I did, they would have been buzzing.) The performers were dazzling—tall figures with extravagant makeup, shimmering outfits, and heels that defied gravity. "Ah," I thought, "Earth women are truly extraordinary!"

It wasn't until later, after a puzzling conversation with another patron, that I realized these performers were called "drag queens"— biological males expressing femininity in vibrant ways. This was my first lesson in the rich tapestry of human gender expression. Note to self: do not assume identity based solely on decorations and clothing.

Venturing further, I met a kind individual who offered companionship in exchange for currency. Assuming this was a customary Earth practice, I eagerly agreed, thinking I was making a new friend. It became clear rather quickly that I had misread the situation. After an awkward farewell, I made a mental note to study the concept of "prostitution" more thoroughly.

Throughout my journey, I've been amazed by the spectrum of femininity on Earth. From the glamorous to the understated, the fierce to the gentle, Earth women embody traits as vast and varied as the galaxy itself.

At a dance gathering, I tried to join in. Let's just say my coordination wasn't up to par. After spilling a few drinks and stepping on someone's toes, a kind woman suggested I "had two left feet." This puzzled me greatly, as I possess the standard number of feet. Earth idioms, it seems, are an adventure all their own.

While I continue my search for a way home, I've embraced my mission to adapt to Earth's culture. Every day brings new challenges, surprises, and opportunities for growth. From the bright streets of Las Vegas to the quiet corners of small towns, I've walked among you, learning and marveling at the complexities of humanity.

So, whether you're a fellow alien trying to make sense of humans or a human seeking a fresh perspective, I invite you to join me on this exploratory voyage. Together, we'll delve into *the* essence of womanhood, celebrate its truths, and maybe even share a laugh or two.

Through my eyes, perhaps you'll see your world in a new light. And who knows? Maybe we'll both learn something about what it truly means to be human.

Buckle up—this is going to be an enlightening ride!

Chapter 1: What Is a Pure Human Female?

Greetings, Earth Friends! On my home planet, the lines between male and female are crystal clear—no confusion, no debates. Our *Gods* shaped our spirits into their image, gifting us the power to create life in ways that are deeply respected and celebrated. It's a divine balance, purposeful and eternal. But here on Earth? Let's just say things are… different. Very different.

In my exploration of Earth women, I've learned that an authentic woman is, at the most basic level, an adult human female. Simple, right? Wrong. This definition barely scratches the surface of how humans define a woman. Here, it seems to be a mix of biology, experience, roles, and an ineffable quality—a kind of spark as unique as the stars in the galaxy. And trust me, asking humans to explain what a "pure human female" is can lead to anything from philosophical debates to near-violent outbursts. Proceed with caution.

Femininity, I've discovered, is not one thing. It's a thousand little things, all woven together into a tapestry of strength and grace. Take Linda, for example. I met her in a picturesque town in the Midwest of the United States. They say Hallmark movies were filmed there, and it felt like stepping into a postcard. The town, called Weston, had a small Italian shop serving some of the most delicious sauces to pair with your noodles—a discovery I highly recommend, by the way.

One sunny afternoon, I wandered into a community garden and found Linda teaching children how to plant vegetables. With dirt smudged on her cheeks and a laugh as warm as sunlight, she guided little hands to dig small holes for seeds. I was just as captivated as the children.

"Just like this," she said gently, tucking a seed into the soil. "We give it a cozy bed, cover it up, and let the earth work its magic."
"Will it really grow?" a wide-eyed girl asked.

"Absolutely," Linda replied with confidence. "With a bit of water and sunshine, it'll sprout in no time."

Linda's nurturing presence and the way she turned gardening into a life lesson fascinated me. Her patience and kindness were shining examples of femininity—an ability to foster growth, both in plants and in curious minds. Watching her, I couldn't help but feel admiration. She wasn't just growing vegetables; she was cultivating potential.

But femininity isn't solely about gentleness. It also manifests in strength and bravery. One evening, I found myself at a local fire station's open house in Salt Lake City, Utah. There, I met Jasmine, a firefighter who radiated resilience.

Jasmine was strong—literally and figuratively. She carried gear so heavy it seemed impossible for anyone, let alone her petite frame, to manage. Intrigued, I asked her, "Are you the only female here? Do you ever need *backup*?"

"Sometimes," she admitted with a smile. "But the fire doesn't care if you're male or female—it just needs to be put out."

Her words carried a simple yet profound truth. Watching her work alongside her team, I realized that femininity and strength aren't opposites; they're partners. Jasmine's courage and determination proved that the essence of being a woman could encompass both compassion and grit.

Eager to understand more, I sought out conversations with women from diverse backgrounds. That's when I met Emily, a scientist who studies the stars—a subject close to my heart.

"Being a woman means pursuing my passions and not letting anyone tell me what I can or can't do," she told me.

"Is that unique to Earth women?" I asked, genuinely curious. "Don't human males pursue their passions too?"

Emily pondered for a moment. "You're right—they do. But historically, women have faced more barriers in fields like science. So, for me, being a woman also means breaking those barriers."

Her *answer* was both enlightening and confusing. On my planet, such limitations don't exist; we all pursue our callings equally. Yet, I admired Emily's resolve and her ability to rise above obstacles. She reminded me that progress often requires perseverance—a lesson applicable to any species.

Perseverance was also a trait I saw in Grace, a stay-at-home mom who invited me to dinner after I attended a small church gathering. Her home was a whirlwind of laughter, tears, and the aroma of freshly baked cookies—a sensory overload, in the best way possible.

"For me, being a woman is about love, sacrifice, and strength," Grace said, handing me a cookie. "Every day is an adventure!"

Her ability to anticipate her children's needs, guide them through chaos, and love them unconditionally struck me as goddess-like. She wasn't just raising a family; she was shaping the future.

While I marveled at the strength and freedom of women like Emily and Grace, I also learned about the challenges women face in other parts of the world. Grace's husband, Sammy, a veteran of Earth wars in Afghanistan and Iraq, told me that in some cultures, women aren't allowed to drive vehicles, make decisions, or even show their faces.

"What's wrong with their faces?" I asked, perplexed.

"Nothing," Sammy said solemnly. "It's just the way things are."

The idea of limiting someone's potential based on their gender was baffling to me. On my planet, we celebrate individuality and encourage everyone to fulfill their divine purpose. Yet, even in the face of such challenges, I've observed Earth women demonstrating resilience and ingenuity. It's both inspiring and humbling.

So, what is a pure human female? She's a partner in creation, a nurturer, a dreamer, a fighter, and a lover. Whether she's teaching in life's classrooms, battling fires, or raising a family, she brings her own brilliance to the world.

But perhaps the most extraordinary trait of human females is their ability to create life. On my planet, the power to give life is held in the highest regard, and witnessing it here on Earth fills me with awe. Isn't it amazing that, as Linda said, you *can* plant a seed, nourish it, and watch it grow to its full potential? One day, humanity will understand the full potential of the human race.

As I continue my journey, I look forward to learning more about the incredible women who make Earth such a vibrant and beautiful place.

Join me in the next chapter as I delve into the biology and psychology that make human females truly remarkable. From anatomy to the mysteries of the mind, this is where science meets wonder.

Chapter 2: The Science of Womanhood

Thank you for staying with me, Earthling! After my initial observations of Earth women—and a few moments of comedic confusion—I decided it was time to approach the subject scientifically. On my planet, the method for creating life, through a sacred union of male and female, is divinely appointed and celebrated. It is both intimate and eternal. Here on Earth, I discovered it is strikingly similar but layered with complexities of biology, psychology, and culture as intricate as the neon lights of Las Vegas. Naturally, I was intrigued.

Human anatomy is nothing short of extraordinary. Armed with a library card (thank you again, Maria!), I ventured into the "Science" section. There, I encountered a diagram labeled "The Female Reproductive System"—a dazzling maze of organs, pathways, and functions. The sheer complexity made me audibly gasp.

"All of this… fits inside a human body?" I muttered, earning a bemused glance from a fellow library patron.

On my planet, the creation of life also begins with the *sacred* union of male and female, but the resulting life is nurtured externally in bio-harbors—carefully monitored environments. Efficient? Yes. Intimate? No. Earth's method, however, places this entire process within the female body. I was astounded. The female body is not only the vessel but also the protector and nurturer of new life. The complexity and beauty of this system filled me with a profound sense of respect for Earth women.

Grace, the remarkable mother I met earlier, helped me understand this on a more personal level. "It's not always easy," she admitted, cradling her youngest child in her arms. "But the sacrifices are worth it. There's nothing like feeling your baby kick for the first time."

The idea of feeling life grow within one's body was foreign to me, but Grace's eyes sparkled with joy as she spoke. This act of co-creation is not merely biological; it's a partnership between male and female and, as Grace reminded me, with the Creator of all life. On Earth, creation is as much a spiritual journey as it is a physical one.

Ah, the hormones! These chemical messengers act as the maestros of the human body, orchestrating a symphony of growth, emotions, and reproduction. Words like "estrogen" and "progesterone" fascinated me as I read about how they influence everything from development to mood.

One day, while observing humans in a bustling corner store, I noticed several women purchasing large quantities of chocolate. Intrigued, I asked one, "Is this for a celebration?"

The woman chuckled. "Let's call it a survival kit for PMS."

Survival? My metaphorical antennae perked up. I purchased a chocolate bar to investigate further. Delicious and intriguing! Humans have developed small indulgences to navigate the challenges of their biology—practical and enjoyable.

The more I learned about Earth women's hormonal cycles, the more I admired their adaptability. On my planet, biological processes are externally regulated with minimal personal impact. Here, women embrace the ebb and flow of their bodies with remarkable resilience, often balancing physical challenges with grace.

Biology alone cannot explain what makes *Earth* women extraordinary. Humans often discuss a quality called "emotional intelligence"—a strength for which women are particularly celebrated. It involves navigating feelings, understanding others, and building connections. On my planet, emotions are analyzed and categorized, filed neatly away for future reference. The human approach, though chaotic, seems to foster deeper relationships and a richer experience of life.

Maria, my ever-patient teacher, explained it best. "Emotions are part of what make us human," she said when I asked how women handle the overwhelming flood of feelings they often encounter.

Her answer puzzled me. Could embracing emotions rather than suppressing them actually make a species stronger? Humans seem to thrive on the connections their emotions create. This ability to navigate feelings with both strength and compassion is a hallmark of Earth women—and perhaps their greatest gift.

One of the most striking aspects of Earth women is their ability to balance strength and sensitivity. Jasmine, the fearless firefighter I mentioned earlier, exemplifies this balance. Watching her confidently carry heavy equipment, extinguish roaring flames, and then return to her community with humility left me in awe.

"How do you balance it all?" I asked her. "You just do what needs to be done," she replied with a shrug. "There's no secret—just heart."

Heart. This concept came up repeatedly in my observations. Earth women seem to have an extraordinary ability to give of themselves, often putting the needs of others before their own. Whether nurturing children, pursuing ambitious careers, or protecting their communities, they approach life with purpose and resolve.

By the end of my exploration, I realized that understanding the science of womanhood requires more than an anatomy chart or a hormonal breakdown. These elements are essential, but they are just the foundation. What truly sets Earth women apart is the fusion of biology, emotional intelligence, and spiritual purpose. They embody resilience, adaptability, and an innate ability to nurture and connect.

The divinely appointed process of creating life—shared by my planet and yours—has an additional layer here on Earth. It's not just a biological event; it's an act of love and creativity, a reflection of the partnership between humans and their Creator. Witnessing this has deepened my respect for the human race and its potential for greatness.

As I write these words, I am filled with gratitude for the women who have shared their stories and their wisdom with me. Earth women are a testament to the beauty of creation, the power of connection, and the strength of the human spirit.

Armed with this foundation of scientific and emotional understanding, I now turn my attention to history. How have the roles and perceptions of women evolved over time? What can Earth's past teach us about its future?

Join me in Chapter 3: Cultural and Historical Perspectives on Women, as I dig deeper into the fascinating story of Earth's pure human female.

Chapter 3: Cultural and Historical Perspectives on Women

After diving into the science of womanhood, I found myself curious about how Earth women's roles have evolved throughout history. On my planet, societal roles *have* remained constant for millennia—structured and predictable. But here on Earth? Your culture is dynamic, evolving at a pace that's as dizzying as your rotating sushi bars. It feels like I'm watching the adolescent development of a species—and trust me, adolescence is a fascinating, albeit awkward, stage.

Determined to understand, I began my quest at the library—a treasure trove of knowledge that costs nothing to enter. Amazing! Thanks to Maria's ingenuity (and my friend Jacob ordering me a piece of mail with his address), I secured a library card. This little piece of plastic opened doors to Earth's vast historical archives.

As I flipped through history books, I uncovered a tale as varied as the stars. In some ancient societies, women were revered as leaders, healers, and even deities. For instance, Cleopatra of Egypt ruled with intellect and influence, leaving a legacy as dazzling as the Nile's golden sands.

But not all societies celebrated women in this way. Many placed women firmly in domestic roles, limiting their influence to the home. It seemed the pendulum of women's status swung wildly over time, shifting between empowerment and restriction.

The suffrage movement particularly caught my attention. Women like Susan B. Anthony stood against societal norms, demanding equality and the right to vote. Their courage reminded me of the resilience I saw in the women living beneath the streets of Las Vegas. It's amazing how the fight for dignity transcends time and *place*.

As I dug deeper, I noticed a recurring theme: the tension between traditional roles and modern opportunities. Historically, women were celebrated as caregivers and nurturers.

Motherhood was considered the pinnacle of womanhood—a role demanding strength, patience, and sacrifice. And rightly so! Raising tiny humans is no small feat.

But as societies progressed, new opportunities opened. Women became astronauts, CEOs, scientists, and artists. Some balanced these ambitions with motherhood; others prioritized one over the other. Either way, the expansion of choices brought new challenges.

I met Karen, a woman typing furiously on her laptop in a bookstore before I got my library card. Curious, I struck up a conversation. I've learned the unfortunate difference between the human female name Karen and "A Karen." I wonder why the name Karen was chosen as a description of particular behavior patterns in people wanted to speak with the manager...?

"Working on something important?" I asked.

"Just trying to finish this project before picking up the kids from school," she sighed. "The juggling act never ends."

"Why do you juggle?" I asked, picturing colorful balls flying through the air.

She laughed. "It's a figure of speech. I mean balancing work and family."

"Ah, I see. On my planet, tasks are automated or assigned based on strengths. We don't expect one person to do everything."

"Well, here, it's kind of expected that women do it all," she said with a wry smile.

The more I observed, the more contradictions I noticed. One day, I stumbled upon an old advertisement from the 1950s. It depicted a smiling woman holding a vacuum cleaner with the caption: "The happiest women are the best homemakers!"
Contrast that with a modern ad promoting a phone app for working mothers, claiming: "You can have it all!"

So which is it? Should women find fulfillment in homemaking, careers, or both? The mixed messages made my head spin faster than my spaceship during its crash landing.

These contradictions aren't just historical; they persist globally. In some places, women are encouraged to pursue STEM fields (Science, Technology, Engineering, and Mathematics—humans love acronyms, and so do I). In others, they're discouraged from receiving any education at all.

I met Fatima, an immigrant from a country where women have limited rights. "Here, I can study to become a doctor," she told me. "Back home, even expressing that desire could put my life at risk."

"That must be liberating," I said.

"It is," she replied. "But sometimes, I still feel the weight of my family's traditional expectations."

It struck me that womanhood on Earth is a complex mosaic, influenced by history, culture, religion, and individual desires. No single narrative can define it.

In my exploration, I encountered two religious young men riding bicycles. They shared their perspective: "Mothers are primarily responsible for nurturing their children."

"That makes sense," I said. "*Good* nurturing requires education, skills, and wisdom to pass on to the next generation."

Their sentiment stayed with me. Whether raising families or breaking barriers, women's roles often center on shaping the future. It's an extraordinary responsibility, requiring strength, resilience, and love.

Reflecting on these cultural and historical perspectives, I realized that defining womanhood is like describing the universe—expansive, varied, and ever-changing. Some women find fulfillment in nurturing families. Others thrive in careers, breaking new ground in their fields. Many do both, juggling their roles with a grace that leaves me in awe.

The key, it seems, is freedom—the freedom for women to choose their own paths without judgment or limitations. As my friend Emily the scientist once said, "The universe is big enough for all of us to shine."

Earth's history reveals both progress and challenges. As I continue my journey, I'm eager to explore the nuances between gender identity and biological sex—a topic that has sparked many questions and, admittedly, some confusion on my part.

Join me in Chapter 4: Gender Identity vs. Biological Sex, as we navigate this intricate and thought-provoking subject together.

Chapter 4: Gender Identity vs. Biological Sex

After exploring the cultural and historical roles of women, I found myself tangled in a particularly complex web of human concepts: gender identity and biological sex. On my planet, these ideas are crystal clear and divinely appointed.

Male and female are harmonious halves of a purposeful whole, with roles rooted in creation and balance. But here on Earth, some humans have made the conversation...complicated.

One fateful afternoon, I was savoring a hot chocolate in a cozy café—a beverage so delightful it must surely be proof of divine inspiration—when I overheard a spirited discussion at a nearby table.

"Gender is a spectrum," declared a young human with vibrant blue hair.

"But biologically, there are only two sexes," countered their companion, adjusting his glasses with scholarly precision.

Curiosity piqued, I leaned over. "Excuse me," I interrupted politely. "Could you help me understand the difference between gender identity and biological sex?"

Their surprise gave way to a warm invitation. "Sure," the blue-haired individual said with a smile. "Pull up a chair."

As they explained, biological sex refers to the physical characteristics that define humans as male or female: chromosomes, hormones, and reproductive organs. Most humans are born with XX chromosomes (female) or XY chromosomes (male), but there are rare variations, such as intersex individuals.

"Think of it as the hardware," said the glasses-wearing human. "It's your physical design."

"Ah, the basic blueprint of the body," I mused, nodding. "Understood."

"Gender identity, on the other hand," continued the blue-haired individual, "is about how someone feels and identifies internally. It's their personal sense of being male, female, both, or neither."

"Fascinating," I said. "So gender is like the software—the programming that runs on the hardware."

They both laughed. "Exactly!"

Eager to deepen my understanding, I sought out individuals willing to share their experiences. At an art gallery, I met Taylor, a talented painter whose work was a vibrant explosion of colors and *text*ures. "Your art is extraordinary," I complimented.

"Thank you," Taylor replied, their eyes lighting up. "It's how I express myself." Taylor shared that they identify as non-binary, meaning they don't exclusively identify as male or female. "For me, gender isn't a box to fit into. It's more like a spectrum of possibilities."

"Does that change how others interact with you?" I asked.

"Sometimes," they admitted. "But I've learned that being true to myself is what matters most."

At a community center, I attended a support group where I met Alex, a transgender man. "What has *your* journey been like?" I asked.

"It's been challenging but fulfilling," Alex shared. "I was born biologically female but always felt male inside. Transitioning was the best decision I ever made, even though not everyone understands or accepts it."

For a more scientific perspective, I visited Professor Jenkins, a psychologist who specializes in human behavior. Her office was cozy, filled with books and models of the human brain.

"Thank you for meeting with me," I began. "I'm trying to understand something called 'gender dysphoria.'"

"Of course," she said kindly. "Gender dysphoria is recognized in the DSM-5, a manual published by the American Psychiatric Association. It describes the distress someone feels when their gender identity doesn't align with their biological sex."

"So, the distress comes from the incongruence?" I asked.

"Exactly," she replied. "This distress can manifest as a strong desire to change one's physical traits or as discomfort with societal expectations tied to their assigned gender."

"Is it considered a mental disorder?" I inquired.

"The term 'disorder' can be misleading," Professor Jenkins explained. "The diagnosis isn't meant to label someone negatively but to help them access care and support."

"So the focus is on alleviating the distress, not the identity itself?"

"Precisely," she affirmed. "The goal is to help individuals live happier, healthier lives."

Despite my growing understanding, I often stumbled. I mistakenly referred to Taylor as "she."

"Actually, I prefer 'they/them,'" Taylor corrected gently.

I couldn't help but wonder: where does this *process* end? How does one navigate the complexities of human identity without making mistakes? And what happens when misunderstandings lead to conflict? As there are only two scientific biological sexes shouldn't the pronouns some people are so passionate about match these?

The more I explored, the more I realized that this topic touches the core of human individuality and society. While biological sex is rooted in physical attributes, gender identity is deeply personal, shaped by feelings, experiences, and culture. Changeable metrics.

I also met many individuals whose gender identities aligned with their biological sex. They seemed grounded, resilient, and confident in their sense of self. I hope those experiencing gender dysphoria can one day find peace in accepting their inherent greatness—their true divine design.

For me, the journey of understanding continues. While I may not fully grasp every nuance, I'm committed to learning and growing with an open mind.

In the next chapter, we'll explore the roles of femininity and motherhood. Together, we'll delve into the nurturing instincts, the profound bond between mothers and children, and how these elements shape societies. Join me as we continue this enlightening adventure!

Chapter 5: Femininity and Motherhood

After navigating the labyrinth of gender identity and biological sex, I felt drawn to explore two of the most revered aspects of Earth womanhood: femininity and motherhood. On my planet, nurturing and creation are considered sacred acts, guided by divine purpose. Here on Earth, I discovered that these roles are equally celebrated but wrapped in layers of complexity, joy, and, at times, profound struggle.

Motherhood on Earth is nothing short of extraordinary. The ability of human females to conceive, carry, and give birth to new life is a process that left me in awe. It's not merely a biological function; it's a partnership with the divine, a testament to the Creator's design, and an emotional journey that shapes the lives of both mother and child.

Having a mother—or even a mother figure—provides innumerable benefits, an *outlined* process of eternal growth. Mothers often serve as a child's first teacher, protector, and source of unconditional love. Their influence is woven into the emotional and psychological foundation upon which individuals build their lives.

From my observations, femininity is often associated with a deep-seated desire to nurture and care for others. While these traits are not exclusive to women, they seem to be central to how many human females express their womanhood. But what does this look like in practice? I sought out stories from Earth women who graciously shared their experiences with me.

In a quaint town surrounded by rolling hills, I met Emma, a mother of three energetic children. We sat on her porch as her youngest chased a butterfly across the yard.

"Motherhood is the most rewarding job I've ever had," Emma said, her eyes shining with pride. "But it's also the hardest."

"How so?" I asked.

"Well, there's the lack of sleep, the constant worry, the balancing act between work and family," she explained. "But then there are moments like this—pure, simple joy—that make it all worthwhile."

"What's the greatest lesson motherhood has taught you?" I inquired.

"Patience," she laughed. "And the ability to love someone more than you ever thought possible."

Back in the underground tunnels of Las Vegas, I reconnected with Sarah, who I first met at the start of my Earthly adventure. Despite facing homelessness, she cared for her two young children with unwavering dedication.

"How do you manage?" I asked as she prepared a modest meal over a small fire.

She smiled softly. "A mother's love knows no bounds. My kids are my world, and I'll do anything to keep them safe."

Her resilience was inspiring. Even in the face of adversity, her maternal instincts guided her every action.

In a shelter for women and children, I met Maria, a single mother who had fled an abusive situation. She was learning new skills to provide for her family.

"Motherhood isn't just about giving birth," Maria told me. "It's about sacrifice, strength, and building a better future for our children."

"What keeps you going during tough times?" I asked.

"My children are my inspiration," Maria said firmly. "Their smiles, their hopes—that's all the motivation I need."

Her words resonated deeply. They made me think of my own mother on my home *planet*. How I missed her comforting presence and wisdom. It was a bittersweet reminder of the universal power of maternal love.

Motherhood is a journey marked by both milestones and challenges—first steps, first words, school graduations, sleepless nights, teenage rebellions, and an ever-present worry that never truly fades.

I spoke with Linda, a mother whose daughter was preparing to leave for college.

"It's bittersweet," Linda admitted. "I'm so proud of her, but it's hard to let go."

"What will you miss the most?" I asked.

"The little moments," she sighed. "Our late-night talks, her laughter filling the house."

"Any advice for new mothers?" I prompted.

"Treasure every moment," she said with a knowing smile. "It goes by faster than you think."

Motherhood is not confined to biological ties. I met Karen, who had adopted two children from overseas.

"People ask if I feel differently because they're not my 'real' children," Karen said, her tone reflecting mild exasperation. "But love isn't defined by genetics."

"What inspired you to adopt?" I inquired. "I always wanted to be a mother," she explained. "When I learned about so many children needing homes, it felt like the right path for me." Similarly, I met Angela, a foster mother who had cared for over a dozen children.

"Each child brings their own challenges and joys," Angela shared. "But providing a safe, loving environment for them, even temporarily, is incredibly fulfilling."

These women embodied the essence of motherhood: love, dedication, and an unyielding commitment to nurturing the next generation.

The benefits of having *a* mother or mother figure are profound. They often provide:

Emotional Support: Comfort during times of distress, helping children navigate their emotions.

Guidance and Mentorship: Teaching life skills, moral values, and social norms.

Unconditional Love: Fostering self-esteem and confidence.

Security and Stability: Creating a sense of safety and belonging.

I met Daniel, a young man who attributed his success to his mother's influence.

"She believed in me when no one else did," Daniel said. "Her support gave me the confidence to pursue my dreams."

While motherhood is a source of immense joy, it also comes with significant challenges:

Societal Pressures: Expectations to be the "perfect" mother can be overwhelming.
Work-Life Balance: Juggling career and family responsibilities is a common struggle.

Single Parenthood: Raising children alone adds financial and emotional strain.

Mental Health: Postpartum depression and anxiety can affect new mothers.

Felicia, a new mother, candidly shared her experience with postpartum depression.

"I felt so guilty for not being overjoyed," she confessed. "It was a dark time, but seeking help made all the difference."

Her openness underscored the importance of supporting mothers, not just in their roles but in their well-being.

Witnessing these stories of love, sacrifice, and resilience deepened my admiration for motherhood. It's a role that shapes individuals and, by extension, entire societies. While femininity and motherhood are deeply intertwined, each woman's journey is unique, reflecting her circumstances, culture, and personality.

As I continue my journey, I am inspired by the incredible women I meet. Their stories remind me of the extraordinary strength and nurturing spirit that defines femininity and motherhood.

In the next chapter, we'll explore how women balance strength with sensitivity. From real-life warriors to compassionate caregivers, we'll see how these qualities coexist in powerful harmony. Join me as we continue this enlightening exploration!

Chapter 6: The Dichotomy of Strength and Sensitivity

As my journey across this fascinating planet continues, I find myself repeatedly marveling at the incredible balance Earth women maintain between strength and sensitivity. It's a delicate dance—a celestial waltz, if you will—that showcases their adaptability and resilience. This harmonious duality is especially evident in the interconnected roles of motherhood and professional endeavors. Intrigued, I decided to delve deeper into this dynamic interplay to uncover how these qualities complement and enhance each other.

You may recall Jasmine, the courageous firefighter I met earlier in my travels. Fascinated by her ability to embody both physical strength and compassionate sensitivity, I decided to visit her fire station for a closer look.

When I arrived, the team was conducting drills, hoisting heavy hoses, and scaling ladders with agility that left me breathless. Jasmine welcomed me with a smile and offered to show me around.

"Being a firefighter requires physical endurance and quick thinking," she explained as we toured the station. "But it's not just about strength. We often encounter people on the worst days of their lives. Compassion is essential."

"Can you give me an example?" I asked, eager *to* understand.

"Well," she said, "handling a tantrum isn't so different from calming someone during an emergency. You need to listen, empathize, and provide reassurance."

Her comparison made me chuckle. "So, being a parent is like being a first responder?"

"In a way, yes," Jasmine agreed. "My experiences as a firefighter have definitely helped me as a mother. When my son fell off his bike and broke his arm, my training kicked in. I stayed calm, assessed the situation, and got him the care he needed without panicking."

Jasmine's story highlighted how professional experiences can enhance parenting skills. Her ability to remain composed under pressure illustrated the seamless integration of strength and sensitivity in both her work and family life.

At the women's shelter where I previously met Maria, I discovered she had formed a close friendship with Grace, the stay-at-home mom and counselor. Together, they exemplified how women support each other in balancing their many roles.

"Maria's determination *is* inspiring," Grace told me during a group activity. "She's balancing work, attending classes, and raising her children." Maria smiled. "Grace has taught me so much about resilience and self-care."

"How do you manage everything?" I asked Maria.

"It's not easy," she admitted. "I prioritize tasks, lean on support networks, and remind myself why I'm doing this—for my kids."

Grace added, "We also attend community workshops on time management and stress reduction. It's amazing how sharing resources can lighten the load."

Their collaboration demonstrated the strength of community and the profound impact of women mentoring and uplifting one another.

Curious about how women manage their wide range of responsibilities, I sought insights from others.

I met Sophia, a project manager and mother of three. "Organization is key," she explained. "I use planners and apps to keep track of everyone's schedules."

"Does that reduce stress?" I asked.

"It helps," she said. "But I've also learned that flexibility is important. Perfection isn't possible."

At a community wellness event, I spoke with Aisha, a nurse who emphasized the importance of self-care. "You can't pour from an empty cup," she said. "I schedule time for myself—whether it's reading, exercising, or simply resting."

"How do you balance that with family and work demands?" I queried.

"By setting boundaries and communicating my needs," Aisha replied. "It's essential for maintaining both strength and sensitivity."

Eager to understand this balance further, I joined a yoga class led by an instructor named Priya. As I struggled to maintain a pose called the "Downward Dog," I toppled over, causing a minor commotion.

Priya approached with a kind smile. "It's okay. Just breathe and try again."

"Is there a position called 'Falling Star'?" I joked, rubbing my elbow.

She laughed softly. "Not yet, but maybe we can create one together!"

Priya's patience and encouragement exemplified sensitivity, while her mastery of the poses demonstrated incredible strength. Her ability to make me feel at ease despite my clumsiness revealed how the two qualities work in harmony.

While exploring career fairs, I met Staff Sergeant Mia Johnson at a military recruitment booth. Her confident demeanor immediately caught my attention.

"Interested in serving your country?" she asked with a friendly smile.

"Perhaps," I replied. "What opportunities does the Army offer?"

"Plenty," Mia said. "From education benefits to career training. The Army develops leadership, discipline, and resilience—skills that are valuable in all areas of life."

As we talked, Mia revealed she was also a mother. "Balancing military service with parenting is challenging, but the Army provides support for families," she said. "And the leadership skills I've gained help me guide my children."

Her words resonated deeply. The idea of joining the military appealed to my desire for structure and purpose. Could this be my next adventure?

Through these encounters, I observed that women employ various strategies to navigate their responsibilities:

Prioritization: Focusing on what matters most in the moment.

Support Networks: Leaning on friends, family, and community resources.

Adaptability: Remaining flexible in the face of challenges.
Self-Compassion: Allowing themselves grace and understanding.

These strategies reflect a remarkable ability to balance strength and sensitivity, seamlessly integrating the two qualities to navigate life's complexities.

From Jasmine's firefighting prowess to Maria and Grace's supportive partnership, and Mia's leadership in both the military and her home, these women illustrate the harmony between strength and sensitivity. Each of their stories deepened my appreciation for the multifaceted nature of womanhood.

Their examples also left me contemplating my own path. Could I embody these qualities in my journey? Maybe I should join the Army. I could learn discipline, resilience, and teamwork while contributing to this nation I've come to admire.

In the next chapter, we'll explore how women navigate the challenges of modern life, balancing career ambitions, family roles, and personal identities. Join me as we continue this enlightening journey!

Chapter 7: Modern Women— Balancing Expectations

Modern human women are a marvel to behold. Watching them balance so many roles— caregiver, professional, dreamer, and sometimes even guppy caretaker—is like witnessing a juggler deftly keep countless balls in the air. Except these balls are much heavier and occasionally unpredictable. Intrigued by this intricate balancing act, I set out to learn more about how Earth women manage the chaos of modern life. It has been remarkable to *follow*.

One sunny morning, I sat in a bustling café, indulging in a comforting cup of hot chocolate— truly one of Earth's greatest inventions. Across the table sat Jasmine, the fearless firefighter and mother of two energetic boys.

"Jasmine, how do you manage being a firefighter and a mom?" I asked, genuinely curious. She chuckled, stirring her coffee. "It's a balancing act, that's for sure. Sometimes I feel like a superhero switching between costumes."

"Do you have a secret identity too?" I whispered conspiratorially.

She grinned. "If only! But seriously, it's about prioritizing what's important and cutting myself some slack when things don't go perfectly." Her words resonated with a theme I was beginning to notice: Earth women often strive for balance without chasing perfection.

Later, I visited Grace and Maria at the women's shelter, where they were organizing a fundraiser to support others in need.

"Maria, you always seem so busy yet so happy," I observed.

She smiled warmly. "I've learned to find joy in the little things. Balancing work, school, and my kids isn't easy, but with support from Grace and others, it becomes manageable."

Grace nodded. "It's about community. We help each other out."

"Like a team?" I asked.

"Exactly!" they replied in unison.

Their partnership showcased the power of leaning on others—a lesson I was learning to appreciate more with each encounter.

Reconnecting with Emily, the brilliant scientist who studies the cosmos, added another layer to my understanding.

"Vega, sometimes I feel like I'm expected to reach for the stars at work and keep my feet firmly on the ground at home," she said, sipping her coffee.

"That sounds… stretchy," I said, imagining her arms elongating cartoonishly.

She laughed. "It's a metaphor. But yes, balancing career ambitions with personal life can be tough."

"How do you do it?" I asked.

"By setting boundaries and remembering why I love what I do," she explained. "Also, coffee helps—a lot."

Curious about the role of self-care, I revisited Aisha's yoga class. This time, I managed not to invent any new poses—though I did wobble a bit.

"Self-care is essential," Aisha told the group. "You can't pour from an empty cup."

I raised my hand. "But if your cup is empty, can't you just refill it?"

She smiled patiently. "Exactly, Vega. Taking time for yourself is how you refill your cup."

"Does that mean I should drink more lattes?" I asked, feigning innocence.

The class chuckled, and Aisha replied, "If that brings you joy, then yes!"

Walking through town one day, I bumped into Staff Sergeant Mia Johnson, the Army recruiter who had *given* me information about military service.

"Hello, Vega! Have you thought more about joining?" she asked.

"I have, but I'm still deciding if it's the right path for me," I admitted.

She nodded. "The military isn't for everyone, but the important thing is finding where you can contribute and grow."

"Mia, how do you balance being a soldier and a mom?" I asked.

"It's challenging," she said, her tone serious. "But discipline and support from my team help. Plus, I make time for my family and hobbies."

"What hobbies?"

"I love painting," she admitted with a smile.

"A soldier and an artist!" I exclaimed.

"Why not?" she laughed. "We all have many sides."

Throughout my conversations, I noticed recurring themes. Modern women juggle their responsibilities with grace by:

Embracing Support: Leaning on friends, family, and community networks.

Prioritizing Joy: Finding happiness in small, meaningful moments.

Being Flexible: Adapting to life's unexpected turns.

Practicing Self-Care: Recognizing the importance of refilling their cups.

Laughing Often: Using humor to lighten heavy burdens.

Inspired by these incredible women, I decided to explore hobbies of my own. During one of Aisha's meditation sessions, I mentioned my newfound love for music.

"That's wonderful, Vega! Why not learn an instrument?" she encouraged.

Taking her advice, I visited a local music shop and picked up a guitar. Strumming in the park, I found myself attracting smiles—and the occasional wince from passersby. "Keep practicing!" one kind jogger called out, her words of encouragement fueling my determination.

I also continued to reflect on the idea of joining the Army. The discipline and camaraderie appealed to me, and perhaps it would provide a sense of purpose during my time on Earth.

Modern women on Earth are like stars in a vast galaxy—each shining uniquely, balancing gravity and light. From Jasmine's firefighting to Grace and Maria's teamwork, Emily's cosmic pursuits, Aisha's teachings on self-care, and Mia's blend of discipline and artistry, their stories have taught me invaluable lessons about navigating life's complexities.

Their strength is not just in their muscles but in their hearts, their ability to adapt, and their willingness to embrace the chaos with a smile.

As I strum my guitar, pondering my next steps, I feel immense gratitude for the women who have shared their wisdom and resilience with me. They've shown me that balance isn't about perfection—it's about finding harmony in life's beautiful chaos.

In the concluding chapter, I'll share my final reflections, hopes, and dreams for Earth and its extraordinary inhabitants. Together, we'll explore how understanding and kindness can make the universe a brighter place.

Chapter 8: Final Thoughts

As I reach the end of this incredible journey through what it means to be a pure human female, I find myself standing at the edge of new adventures. Before we part ways—for now—I want to share some reflections, tease what's next, and perhaps leave you with a bit of mystery to ponder.

When I first crash-landed under the neon lights of Las Vegas, my mission was simple: survival. But along the way, something extraordinary happened—I fell in love with this planet and its incredible inhabitants. Your complexities, your joys, your struggles—they've become a part of my story, and I am forever changed.

I've learned that asking questions is the key to understanding, and so I encourage you: never stop exploring. Whether it's the vastness of the cosmos or the intricacies of your own heart, curiosity is your gateway to growth. The more I observe, the more I see how similar your species is to my own. In fact, with a touch of hair dye, a carefully chosen wig, and some minor skin-tone adjustments, I blend in almost perfectly. I've walked among you, learning from you, marveling at you.

Throughout my travels, I've met extraordinary women who embody strength, sensitivity, and resilience. Jasmine's firefighting bravery, Maria and Grace's community spirit, Emily's cosmic dreams—they've all taught me the power of authenticity and perseverance. They've also shown me the beauty of unity, the kind that comes from shared stories and open hearts.

Now, for those of you ready to go deeper, I will share something I have observed—both through science and spirituality. If you're not prepared to explore these truths, feel free to close the book here, and let us part as cosmic friends. For those who wish to continue, read on.

My race has developed the ability to see and measure matter so fine that mortal eyes cannot perceive it. Through this lens, we've discovered that your spirit—your light, intelligence, and consciousness—is eternal. It was never created, nor can it be destroyed. It is uniquely you.

And here's something astonishing: your mortal body is a reflection of your eternal spirit. Your gender is not just a mortal trait—it is an eternal truth, woven into the very fabric of your being. Whether male or female, this divine identity remains constant, even after your mortal journey concludes.

Your world views existence through the tiniest sliver of eternity, often puzzled by what came before or what lies ahead. But your potential is vast, your purpose immense. There's so much more I wish to share—perhaps in a future book.

Speaking of the future, my journey here is far from over. Recently, I've found solace in music, strumming a guitar under the night sky. Who would've guessed that an alien stranded on Earth would discover a love for songwriting? Perhaps my next adventure will be blending the rhythms of my home planet with Earth's rich musical heritage.

And then there's Mia, the Army recruiter. Our conversation ignited a spark within me. The values of courage, teamwork, and service resonate deeply. I'm considering enlisting—not just to give back to this community but to continue learning and growing alongside others who share a commitment to making a difference.

Reflecting on humanity, I've seen both shadows and light. But what stands out is your incredible capacity for hope, love, and transformation. You have a gift for turning adversity into strength, finding beauty in the mundane, and dreaming beyond the stars. Perhaps Earth holds a unique place in the universe—a beacon of potential, resilience, and unity.

This isn't goodbye; it's merely a pause. I have so many more stories to tell, songs to sing, and insights to share. Keep an eye out for future books, music, or articles where I'll delve even deeper into the wonders of your world and beyond.

Oh, and about my Earth name, Vega Sparx— it's a story wrapped in neon lights and whispered secrets beneath the city streets of Las Vegas. Let's just say it involves a spark (both literal and metaphorical) and a chance encounter that changed everything. But that tale is for another time—a little mystery to keep things interesting!

Before we part ways, I leave you with these thoughts:

Embrace Your Journey: Life is an adventure full of unexpected turns. Each moment shapes who you are becoming.

Foster Connections: Reach out with kindness and openness. You never know whose life you'll touch—or who might transform yours.

Pursue Your Passions: Whether it's art, science, or simply making the best hot chocolate, let your passions guide you.

Look to the Stars, But Live in the Moment: While dreaming of galaxies far away, don't forget the beauty right in front of you.

As I continue my Earthly adventures—perhaps strumming a guitar under the moonlight or donning a uniform to serve—I carry with me the lessons and friendships forged here. Earth has become more than a temporary refuge; it's a home filled with endless possibilities.

So, dear reader, until our paths cross again, keep questioning, keep loving, and keep shining.

The universe is vast, but connections like ours make it feel wonderfully intimate.

With gratitude and a sweet cosmic tune in my heart, warmest embraces,

Vega Sparx

P.S. Stay tuned for more adventures! Whether uncovering the mystery of my name, sharing new music, or diving into the next cosmic question, I promise there's much more to come. After all, the story of Vega Sparx on Earth is just beginning.

The Secret Chapter

Congratulations on making it to the Secret Chapter! You've journeyed through my thoughts, discoveries, and reflections on the fascinating world of Earth and its extraordinary inhabitants. Now, I want to offer you something different—a chance to engage, create, and share your brilliance with me. Think of this chapter as an intergalactic playground, where we can connect across the stars through fun challenges, creative expressions, and meaningful exchanges. Whether you're decoding a hidden message, creating a cosmic doodle, or teaching me something new about your hometown, this is your moment to shine and share your world with an eager alien explorer. Let's have some fun and continue learning from one another. I'm excited to see what you'll come up with!

Cosmic Doodle Challenge

Human talent never ceases to amaze me. Your ability to transform a blank page into something extraordinary is one of the many reasons I admire your species. Now, I present you with an intergalactic competition: the **Cosmic Doodle Challenge.**

The Task:
Draw *me*—Vega Sparx—playing my guitar under the cosmic glow of Earth's stars. Whether you're a seasoned artist or someone who's never doodled before, I challenge you to capture your perception of my physical form and my new musical hobby. Don't worry if you're not "perfect"—on my planet, it's the effort and creativity that matter most.

How to Participate:
1. Use the blank page below to create your doodle.

2. Snap a photo or scan your drawing once it's complete.

3. Share your creation on your favorite social media platform with the hashtag **#VegaSparxGuitarChallenge** so I can find it.

4. Include a short caption about your inspiration—whether it's a favorite part of the book, your love for music, or your vision of the cosmos.

What Happens Next?

I will personally review your cosmic creations. My favorite drawing will earn a *special cosmic reward.* (Spoiler: It might involve exclusive insights about my next adventure!)

Remember:

This isn't just a competition—it's a celebration of your creativity. So grab your pencils, markers, or digital art tools, and let's see how your imagination takes shape!

Doodle Challenge

68

#VegaSparxGuitarChallenge

The Hidden Message Challenge (easy)

Welcome to the next layer of discovery, Earthling! On my planet, scholars often enjoyed deciphering hidden messages embedded within texts. These weren't just puzzles—they were opportunities to uncover deeper truths and refine one's intellect. I've brought a simpler version of this practice to you as a challenge. Let's see if the human race is up for it!

How It Works

Below is a coded message. Your mission is to decode it. If you succeed, you'll unlock a special insight that only the most dedicated readers will uncover.

The answer is hidden in plain sight within the book. If you think you've cracked the code, keep the answer a secret! Instead of sharing it widely, email me at **vega.sparx@vegasparx.com**. I'll let you know if you're correct! If you can crack this code, I might just include a more complex version in my next book.

Your Test:

___ ___ ______ ___ ______.

______ ___ ______ _______ __ __

____ ____.

___ ____ ___ _____ ___ ___ ______.

____ ______ ____ __ _ ____ _____

__ _____.

Hint (there will be no hint like this next time)…
6, 18, 15, 12, 22.
52, 12, 35, 38, 9, 20, 33.
12, 13, 25, 55, 6, 12, 16.
33, 40, 7, 47, 41, 29, 26, 46, 3.

Teach Vega Challenge: Share the Wonders of Your Hometown

I've come to marvel at the diversity and uniqueness of Earth's towns, cities, and hidden gems. While I've explored places like Las Vegas and small Midwestern towns, I know I've only scratched the surface of your incredible world. That's where YOU come in!

I need your help to teach me more about Earth by introducing me to the special treasures of your hometown. It could be a place where you love to eat (what do you call them... "diners"? "Food trucks"?), a quiet park that brings you peace, or even a quirky landmark that every visitor MUST see. Perhaps it's a hidden hiking trail, a favorite bookstore, or the best spot to catch a sunset.

Here's your mission:

Think of a place, activity, or tradition from your hometown that you think I, Vega Sparx, absolutely need to know about.

Share a photo, a description, or a fun fact about it on social media.

Use the hashtag #TeachVega so I can easily find your post and learn from you!

Bonus points if you add a short explanation of why this place or tradition is meaningful to you.

Imagine me, Vega Sparx, exploring your favorite hidden gem, strumming my guitar by that quiet lake, or trying your favorite meal from the local food joint. You'll be helping an alien expand his understanding of your world while spreading a little pride and joy about your hometown to the human race!

I'll be selecting some of my favorite submissions to feature in an upcoming project—so get creative! Who knows? Your suggestion could inspire my next big Earth adventure.

Let's make this planet feel even more like home, one hometown wonder at a time. I'm counting on you to teach me something extraordinary. Remember: #TeachVega.

Thank you for diving into the Secret Chapter and joining me in these creative challenges! You've helped me see Earth in new and exciting ways, and I hope you've had as much fun participating as I've had sharing my adventures with you. From cosmic doodles to secret codes to teaching me about your hometown, your contributions make this journey even more special. Remember, the connections we forge—whether through art, puzzles, or shared stories—are what bring the universe closer together. Keep shining your unique light, and who knows? Perhaps one day we'll meet under the stars, strumming guitars, or exchanging stories in person. Until then, keep exploring, creating, and teaching. You are, after all, the greatest wonder of this planet.